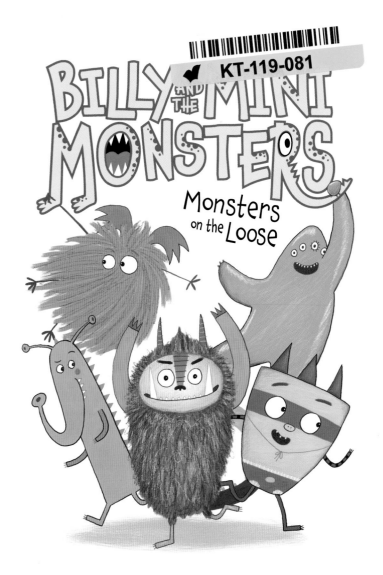

BILLY AND THE MINI MONSTERS

Monsters on the Loose

ZANNA DAVIDSON

Illustrated by
MELANIE WILLIAMSON

Reading consultant: Alison Kelly

Meet Billy...

Billy was just an ordinary boy living an ordinary life, until **ONE NIGHT** he found five **MINI MONSTERS** in his sock drawer.

Gloop   Peep   Fang-Face   Captain Snott   Trumpet

Then he saved their lives, and they swore never to leave him.

We give you the Secret-Hairy-Snot-Tooth Oath of Devotion.

We're awesome!

And fun!

And SCARY!

Are we scary? I'm not sure I'm very scary.

One thing was certain – Billy's life would never be the same AGAIN...

Contents

Chapter 1
The Hound of Death
5

Chapter 2
Out of the Bag
18

Chapter 3
The Flying Hamster
30

Chapter 4
The Flying Potato
46

Chapter 5
Missing
62

Chapter 6
Bully No More
72

Chapter 1
The Hound of Death

Billy and his Mini Monsters had been very busy all week. So far they had flown to **outer** space...

and played a lot of...

hide-and-seek.

"And for our next adventure," announced Captain Snott, "we'd like to go to school with you, Billy."

"**No way**," said Billy. "It's far too dangerous for you and you'll get me into serious trouble!"

Here are some of the things Billy was worrying about:

Captain Snott showing off

Fang-Face eating everyone's ties

Gloop getting stuck

Trumpet's cheese-powered farts

PARP!

And, worst of all, the Mini Monsters being discovered and put in a...

ZOO

"But we could scare off Basil Brown, your school bully," suggested Fang-Face. "He's sounds nastier and nastier every time you talk about him."

I'll show him!

Billy shook his head. "No one could scare Basil Brown. He's the

BIGGEST,

MEANEST,

BADDEST

boy in school.
He'd eat you for breakfast."

"If you leave us here, your new puppy will **EAT US** for breakfast," whispered Peep. "That would be even more dangerous than school."

The puppy?

Yes. The scary, scary puppy!

"To you it's a sweet little dog," Captain Snott explained to Billy. "To us, it is the **HOUND OF DEATH**."

"Don't be silly," said Billy. "I'll take her downstairs before I go. You'll be fine."

15

16

Chapter 2
Out of the Bag

"I'm glad the Mini Monsters are safe at home," thought Billy.

"I've got
enough to worry
about with Basil—"

Aaaaargh!

"Oh no," groaned
Billy, as the
Mini Monsters

s c a t t e r e d

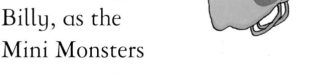

in all directions.

19

How on earth **was he going to find them?**

They could be lost in the school

FOR EVER!

"I'll wait until everyone else has gone into the classroom," Billy decided. "Then I'll look for them."

"Good morning, Billy," said his teacher, Mr. Parker, coming up behind him.

In you go, please.

Billy HAD to go into the classroom.

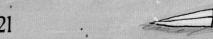

But as he went in, something on the floor caught his eye. Something small and HAIRY.

Peep!

Billy quickly bent down to pick him up.

22

"Billy! What have you got in your hands?" asked Mr. Parker.

"Show me," his teacher said.

Billy froze.

Where could he hide Peep? There was nowhere to put him...

...nowhere except the **HAMSTER CAGE.**

"Look, Mr. Parker!" said Billy.

I've got empty hands.

26

27

28

29

Chapter 3
The Flying Hamster

Billy sat in worried silence all through the register. Then...

"Mr. Parker," said Basil Brown.

I think the hamster's had a baby.

"It's true," said Basil. "I can see them. Actually, the new hamster looks like it's got... **wings**."

Mr. Parker started to walk over.

Billy knew he had to do something — *and fast.*

"Don't go near it!
It's…
it's… **DEADLY**."

A deadly hamster?

"Yes," replied Billy, getting desperate. "I brought it from home. It's got, um, **POISONOUS FUR**! You can't go near it."

"Don't be ridiculous!"
said Mr. Parker, as he went to
open the hamster cage.

Billy gulped. He didn't know
what to do. If Peep was found…

Then he heard a strange noise.

Slurp! Squelch! Slurp!

Billy looked up.

Oh no!

SPLAT!

Gloop landed on
Mr. Parker's head.

Aaargh!

Mr. Parker screamed and
leapt into the air.

Billy took
his chance. He
grabbed Peep from
the hamster cage…
and put him in his
pencil case.

By now, Gloop was oozing his way down Mr. Parker's back.

"Get it off me!" cried Mr. Parker, jumping around the classrom.

"There's a **GIANT SLUG** under my shirt."

"I'll help!" said Billy.

He *rushed* up to Mr. Parker, grabbed Gloop and darted back to his seat.

A strange **hush** fell over the classroom. Basil Brown looked at Billy suspiciously.

"Where's the slug?" asked Basil Brown.

"Oh," said Billy. "I'll, er… just throw him out the window."

"And what's happened to the other hamster?" Basil Brown went on. "It's not there any more."

The whole class looked at Billy.

Billy?

It was a joke?

But there were TWO hamsters, I saw them.

"Maybe you need glasses?" said Billy.

Mr. Parker strode over to inspect the hamster cage. "There's definitely only one hamster here, Basil. Let's get on with our lesson, shall we? And *no* more jokes, Billy." He still looked quite upset about the giant slug.

I'm watching you, Billy.

42

43

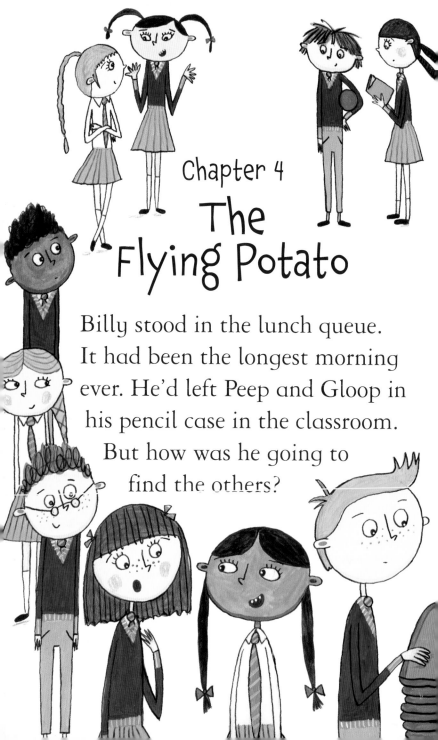

Chapter 4
The Flying Potato

Billy stood in the lunch queue. It had been the longest morning ever. He'd left Peep and Gloop in his pencil case in the classroom. But how was he going to find the others?

Then he heard a small parp,
followed by a **TERRIBLE** smell.

Only one creature in the world
could smell that bad…

Trumpet?

"There he is!" Billy thought with relief. "I'll just ask for that potato. I'm so close now…"

TOO LATE.

Basil Brown was reaching across for the plate… Now he had Trumpet on his tray.

If Billy didn't do something, Basil was going to **EAT** Trumpet.

"Actually," said Billy, in a small voice. "I wouldn't eat that potato, if I were you. I saw a… um… er… spider on it."

"I don't believe you," Basil said. "You're acting really weird today." Then, to Billy's **HORROR**, Basil glanced down at his plate…

As Basil reached for the lettuce leaf to look for the spider, Billy grabbed the plate.

Trumpet…whirled through the air

and landed…

SPLOSH

…in the baked beans.

The potato collided…

SPLAT

…with Basil's face.

"Help!" cried Trumpet, his voice a small squeak.

He tried to swim, but the sauce was too sticky. He slowly, slowly began to S I N K into the beans...

The next moment, Trumpet **disappeared** from view.

Billy pushed past Basil
and plunged his arms
into the baked beans
frantically
trying
to find
TRUMPET.

"WHAT are you doing?" thundered Mr. Parker.

Billy leaped back, dripping baked beans everywhere.

You are in **BIG** trouble, Billy. Return to the classroom at once!

Mr. Parker walked Billy back to his classroom. "I am going to have to talk to your parents about this," he said. "I don't know what's got into you today, Billy."

Billy waited until Mr. Parker had gone. Then he slowly opened his hand. "Trumpet?" he whispered.

Trumpet grinned at him, nodding.

"And I've still got my **cheese**!" he said.

Gloop and Peep peered out of Billy's pencil case. "Trumpet!" they said.

"Isn't this fun?" said Gloop.

Billy put his head in his hands. "I am in so much trouble. Basil will NEVER forgive me."

"And I've still got TWO monsters to find. What if I never find Captain Snott and Fang-Face? They could be

ANYWHERE!"

61

Chapter 5
Missing

The rest of the day passed **very slowly.**

Mr. Parker was still cross about the baked beans. And the GIANT slug.

Basil Brown was furious about the baked potato.

And the **MYSTERY** hamster.

Worst of all, Billy had **no idea** where Fang-Face was.

And he couldn't go home without him.

Billy looked for him during PE.

He wasn't in the school
gym… But Basil Brown was.

At breaktime, Billy
looked for Fang-Face
EVERYWHERE.

In the science lab

In the music room

In the dining hall

In the computer room

Fang-Face was
nowhere to be found.

Finally, Billy went to the playground. And at that point, he knew…

There was no escaping

BASIL BROWN.

Ha! Got you... and with no teachers near.

Everyone gathered round.

"You lied about the hamster," said Basil. "You threw a potato in my face."

Now you'll be sorry.

I have to HELP Billy!

Chapter 6
Bully No More

Billy found Basil crouched in a corner of the playground, hiding from the other children.
Billy couldn't believe it.

"You're not at all scary, are you?" Billy said to Basil.

"Wh-wh-what was that thing?" Basil asked. He was still shaking.

"He's my pet **MONSTER**, Fang-Face," said Billy, grinning.

All the way home from school, Billy's mum told him off.

The teacher said you got baked beans all over the dining hall!

And threw a baked potato!

What were you thinking? **No TV** for a week!

But Billy didn't mind. He knew he'd NEVER feel scared of Basil Brown, ever again.

As soon as he got to his bedroom, Billy took out the Mini Monsters.

"You were **awesome**!"

"Can we go to school again tomorrow?" asked Fang-Face.

Er... maybe not tomorrow.

Captain Snott grinned. "I don't think we need to be scared of it again, either."

All about the
MINI MONSTERS

FANG-FACE →

LIKES EATING:
socks, school ties,
paper, or anything
that comes his way.

SPECIAL SKILL:
has massive fangs.

**SCARE FACTOR:
9/10**

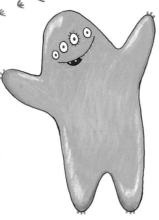

← GLOOP

LIKES EATING: cake.

SPECIAL SKILL:
very stre-e-e-e-tchy.
Gloop can also swallow
his own eyeballs and
make them reappear on
any part of his body.

**SCARE FACTOR:
4/10**

CAPTAIN SNOTT

LIKES EATING: bogeys.

SPECIAL SKILL:
can glow in the dark.

SCARE FACTOR: 5/10

PEEP

LIKES EATING: very small flies.

SPECIAL SKILL: can fly (but not very far, or very well).

SCARE FACTOR: 0/10 (unless you're afraid of small hairy things)

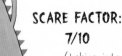

TRUMPET

LIKES EATING: cheese.

SPECIAL SKILL: amazingly powerful cheese-powered parps.

SCARE FACTOR: 7/10 (taking into account his parps)

Series editor: Becky Walker
Edited by Lesley Sims and Becky Walker
Designed by Brenda Cole
Cover design by Hannah Cobley

Digital Manipulation by John Russell

First published in 2017 by Usborne Publishing Ltd., Usborne House,
83-85 Saffron Hill, London EC1N 8RT, England. www.usborne.com
Copyright © 2017 Usborne Publishing Ltd. UKE